The Key to the Cupboard

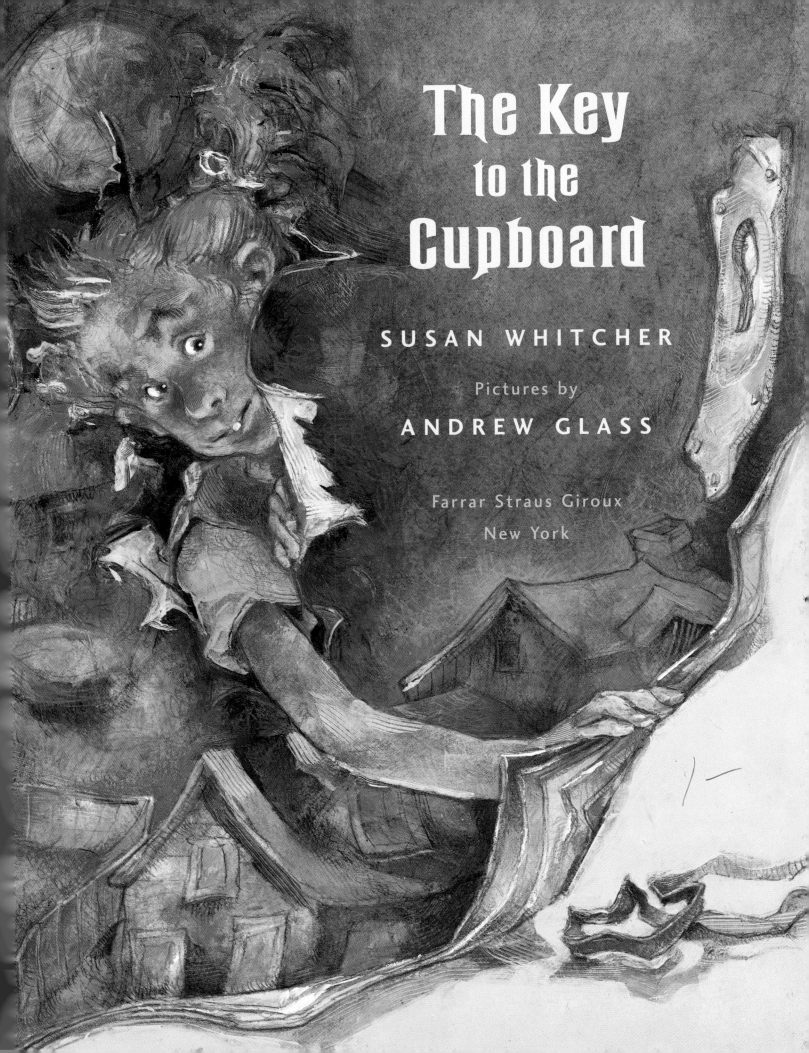

The Key to the Cupboard

SUSAN WHITCHER

Pictures by

ANDREW GLASS

Farrar Straus Giroux

New York

For Susannah, who let me borrow her witch —S.W.

For D. J. —A.G.

Text copyright © 1997 by Susan Whitcher

Pictures copyright © 1997 by Andrew Glass

All rights reserved

Published simultaneously in Canada by HarperCollins*Canada*Ltd

Color separations by Hong Kong Scanner Arts

Printed and bound in the United States of America by Worzalla

Typography by Filomena Tuosto

First edition, 1997

Library of Congress Cataloging-in-Publication Data

Whitcher, Susan.

The key to the cupboard / Susan Whitcher ; pictures by Andrew Glass. — 1st ed.

p.   cm.

Summary: Alice Snavely, the witch who resides in the cupboard under the stairs, leads
a child on a night flight and a confrontation with a wizard.

ISBN 0-374-34127-3

[1. Witches—Fiction. 2. Wizards—Fiction.] I. Glass, Andrew, ill. II. Title.

PZ7.W5774Ke   1996

[Fic]—dc20   95-39842

In a dark corner under the stairs at our house is a cupboard that no one can open. The key fell into a crack in the floor, and no one can get it out. Except me.

Inside the cupboard, another flight of stairs
goes up to a room with a window.

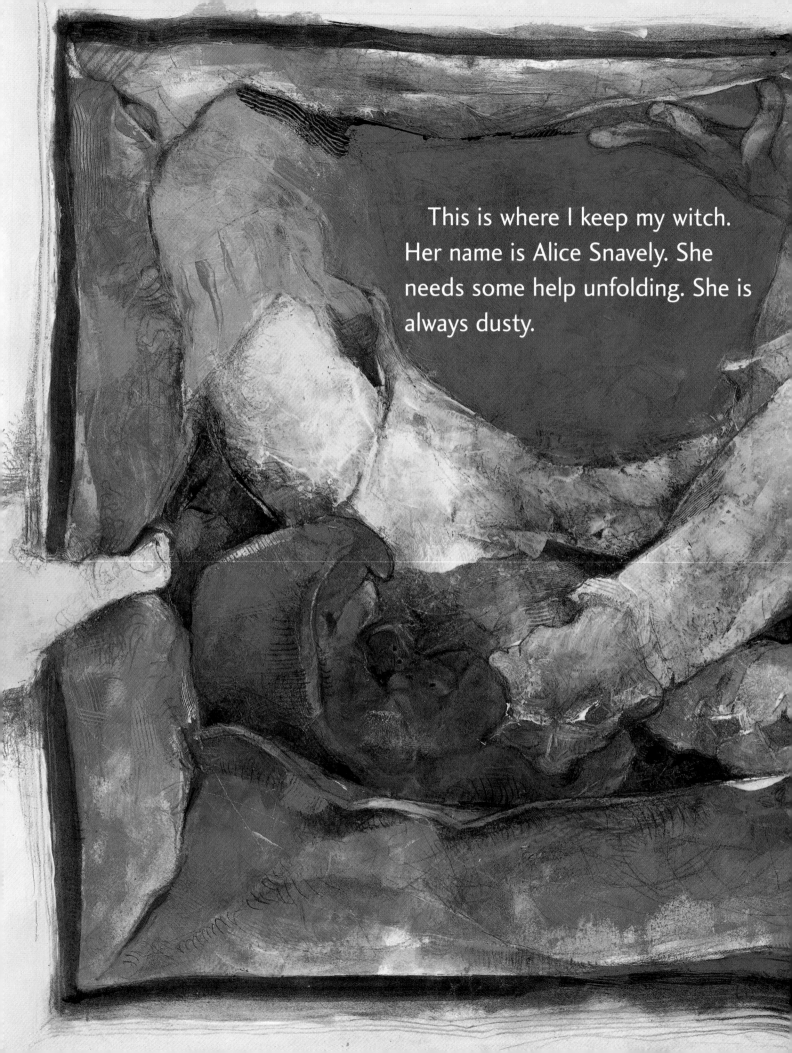

This is where I keep my witch. Her name is Alice Snavely. She needs some help unfolding. She is always dusty.

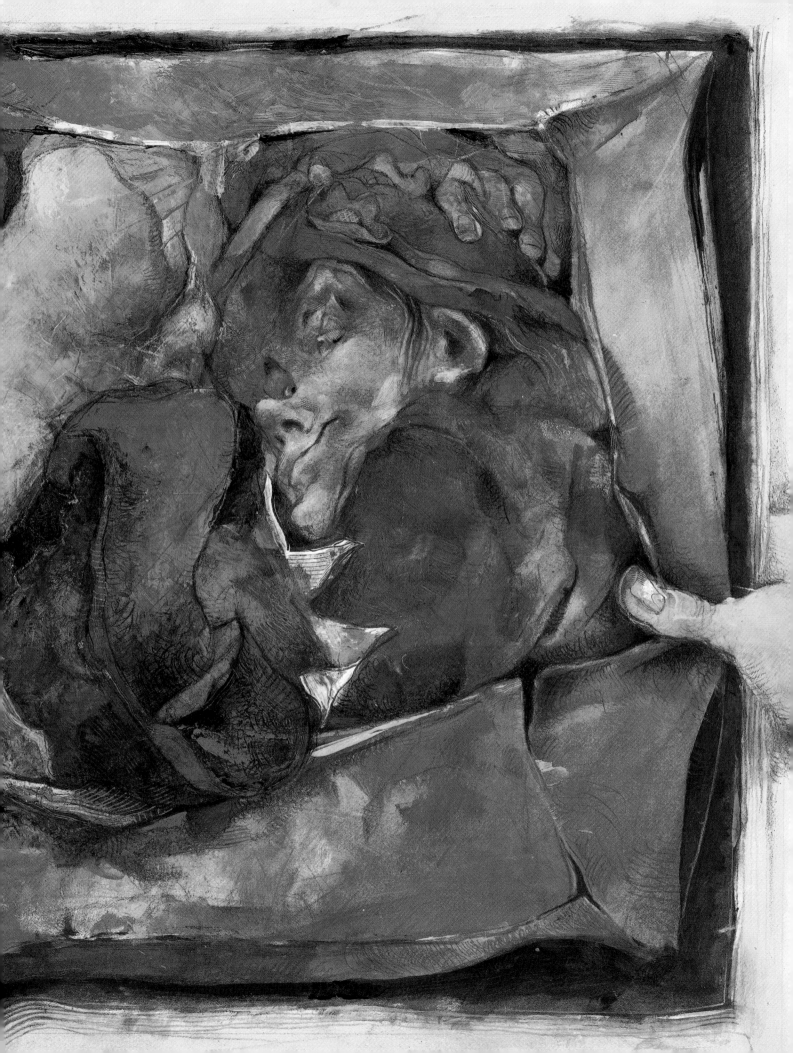

We get out the caldron and make brew. She puts in bats' teeth and bee stings and spit. I put in marshmallows and purple ink and birthday candles with the wishes still in them. We push all the cardboard boxes and junk out of the way so there is room to dance.

My witch weaves the steam with snaky thin fingers.

Our brew is terrifically
powerful. Three drops
Drip! *Drop!* POP!
on the tip of the broom make
the bristles twitch and hop.
The cat's whiskers stand
out like lightning bolts.

Then we are ready to go out
of the window where it is almost
always night.

A full moon and a rising wind make racing
shadows on the lawn below. The shadows leap
and reach out. Three drops
Drip! *Drop!* POP!
of the witch's brew and they change
into long-necked birds and knights on
galloping horses, and a wizard with
a beard.

The wizard's beard spills out of his helmet like
a river. It flows over his knees and drips down
the ribs of his black horse. The night wind
riffles the beard. We see the magic
in it, glinting.

I warn my witch not to touch.
This wizard is too dangerous to
tease. But Alice is reaching for
the glinting beard.
Watch out!
He seizes Alice by the ankle and
tips us toppling into the swirling river.

Drip! *Drop!*
One of my witch's shoes is good for a boat. She steers us carefully toward the bank. We wade ashore.

Alice is tangled in a waterweed.
It holds her by one bony ankle. We
tug and tug—
POP!
The gleaming weed is a strand
of hair.

Three drops
Drip! *Drop!* POP!
and we have a horse quick and
light as a leaf on the wind.

We race for home. Alice flings her strand of
wizard's beard into the air. It comes down
slowly, unwinding into a staircase.

We race up the stairs, up and up,
around and around, until we come
to the open window. The wizard is
six steps behind. Three more drops
Drip! *Drop!* POP!

and the hair tumbles down. The wizard drops
PLOP!
on the ground. I bang the window shut. Alice
Snavely shakes a snaky finger at the wizard
sulking outside in the moonlight.

She tells me to start saving eggshells. She has a spell to rob that wizard of his troublesome beard.

I help my witch fold up again. The river has made her dust damp. Next time, she will be very wrinkled. But she winks her little red eye at me before I put down the lid. She has great plans for those eggshells.

I follow the stairs back to the
cupboard that no one can open
because the key

is carefully lost in a crack in the floor. And it is almost time for supper.

Drip! *Drop!*

POP!